The No. 1 Ladies' Detective Agency

ALEXANDER McCALL SMITH

Level 3

Retold by Anne Collins
Series Editors: Andy Hopkins and Jocelyn Potter

Pearson Education Limited
Edinburgh Gate, Harlow,
Essex CM20 2JE, England
and Associated Companies throughout the world.

ISBN-10: 1-4058-3396-3
ISBN-13: 978-1-4058-3396-7

This edition first published by Penguin Books 2006

Text copyright © Penguin Books 2006
Illustrations by Doreen Lang

Typeset by Graphicraft Limited, Hong Kong
Set in 11/14pt Bembo
Printed in China
SWTC/01

Produced for the Publishers by
Graphicraft Productions Limited, Dartford, UK

Published by Pearson Education Limited in association with
Penguin Books Ltd, both companies being subsidiaries of Pearson Plc

For a complete list of the titles available in the Penguin Readers series, please write to your local
Pearson Education office or to: Penguin Readers Marketing Department, Pearson Education,
Edinburgh Gate, Harlow, Essex, CM20 2JE, UK

Contents

Introduction

'Women understand what's happening. They are the ones with eyes.'

Mma [Mrs] Precious Ramotswe is a kind, warm-hearted – and large – African lady. She is also very unusual. She is the only lady private detective in Botswana and her agency, The No. 1 Ladies' Detective Agency, is the best. With the help of her secretary, Mma Makutsi, and her good friend Mr JLB Matekoni, she solves a number of difficult – and sometimes dangerous – problems.

A stolen car, a missing finger or a missing husband – Mma Ramotswe will solve all these mysteries in her own special way. Her way of working is very different from famous detectives like Sherlock Holmes. But she, too, is very successful.

Alexander McCall Smith was born in Zimbabwe. He went to school there and in Scotland. Like Mma Ramotswe, he is a very interesting and unusual person. He has written more than fifty books – not only books on subjects like criminal law, but also books for children and short stories. He is a wonderful storyteller.

Alexander McCall Smith now lives in Scotland, but he has taught at different universities in Africa. He lived in Botswana for some time, working on criminal law. He loves writing about Africa, and African people. His stories are always full of colour and life. One day he saw a fat Batswana lady running after a chicken for a meal. She gave him the idea for Mma Precious Ramotswe.

Botswana is a country where change has happened very fast. Many of the old African ways are disappearing as it becomes a modern country. Mma Ramotswe misses the old ways, but she is proud to be a modern lady too. Today Botswana's first lady private detective is popular all around the world.

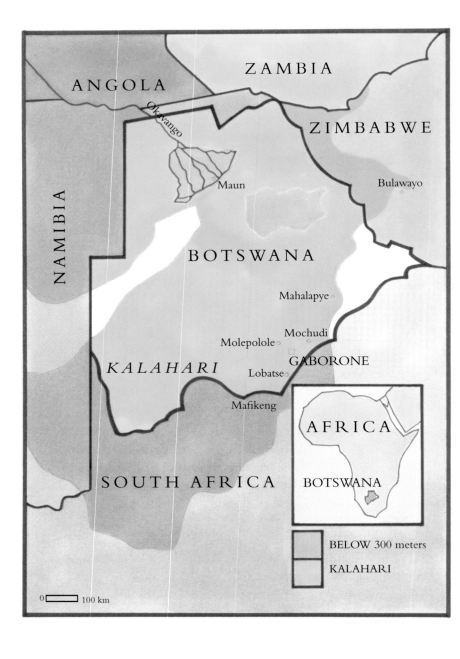

Chapter 1   The Daddy

Mma Precious Ramotswe had a detective agency in Africa, at the foot of Kgale Hill. She was the only lady private detective in Botswana, and her agency was the best. So she called it the No.★1 Ladies' Detective Agency.

Mma Ramotswe was a good detective and a good woman. She loved her country, Botswana, and she loved Africa too. The people of Africa were her people, her brothers and sisters. She wanted to help them solve the mysteries in their lives, so she became a private detective.

The detective agency was in a small building in the town of Gaborone. Outside the building was a sign:

THE NO. 1 LADIES' DETECTIVE AGENCY.
FOR ALL PRIVATE BUSINESS.

The agency had a tiny white van, two desks, two chairs and an old typewriter. There was also a teapot, and three large cups – one for Mma Ramotswe, one for her secretary and one for the client.

In front of the agency was a tree. When Mma Ramotswe was not busy, she loved to sit under this tree. It was a very good place to think. She could look across the dusty road to the town and, far away, she could see the blue hills. Hills in Botswana always looked blue in the heat.

Mma Ramotswe thought about many things while she was sitting under the tree. She thought about her father, and the beginning of the No. 1 Ladies' Detective Agency.

Mma Ramotswe's father worked in the mines in South Africa

★ no. : short for *number*

1

for fifteen years. The mines were very dangerous. Rocks fell and killed men. The dust destroyed their health.

Mma Ramotswe's father saved the money from his years in the mines and bought one hundred and eighty fine cattle. But the dust from the mines was still in his body and he became ill.

'I want you to have your own business,' he said to Mma Ramotswe on his death bed. 'Sell the cattle and buy a business. A shop, perhaps?'

Mma Ramotswe held her father's hand and looked into his eyes. She loved her father, her Daddy, more than anyone in the world. Now he was dying. It was difficult to talk through her tears.

'I'm going to start a detective agency,' she said. 'Down in Gaborone. It will be the best agency in Botswana. The No. 1 Agency.'

Her father's eyes opened wide with surprise. 'But . . . but . . .'

But he died before he could say anything more.

◆

The No. 1 Ladies' Detective Agency became very successful. At first business was slow, but then more and more clients came. One of Mma Ramotswe's first clients was Happy Bapetsi.

'I have been lucky in my life,' said Happy Bapetsi as she drank tea in Mma Ramotswe's office. 'But then this thing happened.'

Mma Ramotswe watched Happy Bapetsi's face carefully. Happy Bapetsi was an intelligent woman. She also had few worries – there were no worry lines on her face.

'It is probably some trouble with a man,' thought Mma Ramotswe. 'A man has come into this woman's life and destroyed her happiness.'

'I grew up in Maun, up near the Okavango River,' said

Happy. 'My mother had a small shop. We had lots of chickens and we were very happy.

'My Daddy left home when I was still a baby. He went to work in Bulawayo, up in Zimbabwe, and he never came back. So my mother and I decided that he was probably dead. But I wasn't sad about my Daddy because I didn't remember him.

'I did well in my school examinations. After I left school, I got a good job in a bank. Now I am thirty-eight years old, I earn a lot of money and I have a nice house with four rooms. I am very happy.'

Mma Ramotswe smiled. 'You have done well,' she said.

'But then this thing happened,' said Happy Bapetsi. 'My Daddy arrived at the house.'

Mma Ramotswe was surprised. So it was not a problem with a boyfriend. It was a problem with a father.

'He just knocked on the door,' said Happy Bapetsi. 'It was a Saturday afternoon and I was taking a rest on my bed. I got up and went to the door. A man of about sixty years old was standing there with his hat in his hands.

'I am your Daddy,' he said. 'Can I stay with you?'

'He told me my mother's name. I was very surprised but I was also excited. My mother was dead. I was happy to meet my Daddy. I made a bed for him in one of the rooms and cooked him a large meal of meat and vegetables. He ate it very quickly and then he asked for more.

'That was about three months ago. Since then, he has lived in that room and I have done all his work. I make his breakfast, cook lunch for him, and then supper at night. I buy him one bottle of beer a day and I have also bought him some new clothes and a pair of good shoes. He just sits in his chair outside the front door and gives me orders.'

'Many men are like that,' said Mma Ramotswe.

'Yes,' Happy Bapetsi agreed. 'But I don't think that this man is my real Daddy. Perhaps he heard about our family from my real Daddy before he died. So he came to Botswana. He has found a very good home for himself.

'Can you help me? Can you find out if this man is really my Daddy? If he is, then he can stay with me. But if he is not, then I want him to leave.'

'Yes,' said Mma Ramotswe. 'I'll find out.'

All that day, Mma Ramotswe thought about Happy Bapetsi's Daddy. How could she find out if he was the Daddy or not? She thought for a long time, then she had an idea.

Mma Ramotswe had a friend who was a nurse. This friend was a large lady, like Mma Ramotswe. Mma Ramotswe borrowed her friend's clothes, and put them on. She looked just like a real nurse. Then she drove to Happy Bapetsi's house in her tiny white van.

The Daddy was sitting in his chair outside the front door, enjoying the morning sun. Mma Ramotswe stopped the car and ran quickly up to the house.

'Are you Happy Bapetsi's Daddy?' she said.

The Daddy stood up. 'Yes,' he said proudly.

'I'm very sorry, but Happy has been in a car accident,' said Mma Ramotswe. 'She is very ill in the hospital.'

'My daughter!' cried the Daddy. 'My little baby, Happy!'

'Yes,' Mma Ramotswe continued. 'Happy is very sick, and she has lost a lot of blood. We must get more for her.'

'Yes,' said the Daddy. 'They must give her that blood. Lots of blood. I can pay.'

'The money is not a problem,' said Mma Ramotswe. 'Blood is free, but we don't have the right kind. We will have to get blood from someone in her family, and you are the only person. We must ask you for some blood.'

The Daddy sat down heavily. 'I am an old man,' he said.

'Yes,' said Mma Ramotswe. 'That is why we are asking you.

Happy needs a lot of blood, so we will have to take about half your blood. It will be very dangerous for you.'

'Dangerous?' said the Daddy.

'Yes,' said Mma Ramotswe. 'But you are her father. We know that you will want to help your daughter. Now come quickly or it will be too late.'

The Daddy opened his mouth and closed it again.

'Come with me,' said Mma Ramotswe, taking his wrist. 'I'll help you to the van.'

'No,' said the Daddy in a weak voice. 'I can't go. I am not really her Daddy. There has been a mistake.'

'You are not her Daddy?' said Mma Ramotswe angrily. 'Then why are you sitting in that chair and eating her food? Do you know that there is a law in Botswana against people like you?'

The Daddy looked down at the ground and shook his head.

'Go inside that house and get your things,' said Mma Ramotswe. 'You have five minutes. Then I am going to take you to the bus station and you are going to get on a bus and never come back.'

When Happy Bapetsi returned home, the Daddy's room was empty. There was a note from Mma Ramotswe on the kitchen table. As Happy read the note, she smiled.

That man was not your real Daddy. He told me. Maybe you will find your real Daddy one day. Maybe not. But now you can be happy again.

Chapter 2   Note Makoti

Mma Ramotswe grew up in a small village called Mochudi. When she was very young, her mother died in a terrible accident. So a cousin of her father's came to look after the little girl. The cousin made her clothes, took her to school and cooked meals for Precious and her father.

The cousin wanted Precious to be clever, so she taught her to count. They counted cattle and trees and boys playing in the dust. She helped Precious remember lists of things – the names of people in her family and the names of cattle. When Precious went to school, she knew the letters A–Z and her numbers up to two hundred. She also knew a few words of English.

Every Sunday, Precious went to Sunday school at the church. There she learned about the difference between right and wrong. She understood this very well. It was wrong to lie. It was wrong to steal. It was wrong to kill other people.

When Precious was eight, the cousin got married. Her husband was a good, kind man and he was rich too. He owned two buses. After the wedding, the cousin and her husband went to live in a house sixteen kilometres south of Gaborone. The cousin wrote letters to Precious.

I know you are missing me. But I know too that you want me to be happy. I am very happy now. I have a kind husband who has bought me wonderful clothes. One day, you will come and stay with me, and we can count the trees again and sing. Now you must look after your father. He is a good man too.

At the age of sixteen, Precious left school. 'She is the best girl in this school,' said the Head Teacher. 'One of the best girls in Botswana.' Her father wanted her to stay at school, but Precious was bored with the small village of Mochudi. She wanted to go somewhere. She wanted her life to start.

'You can go to my cousin,' her father said. 'That is a different place. You will find lots of things happening in that house.'

He felt sad when he said this. He wanted Precious to stay and look after him, but that was selfish. Precious wanted to be free. She wanted to feel that she was doing something with her life.

Her father was worried about men too. 'There are a lot of bad men in the world,' he thought. 'Perhaps Precious will choose the wrong kind of husband.'

The cousin was pleased to have Precious in the house, and she gave her a bright, comfortable room. Precious was given a job in the office of the bus company. She had to check the numbers in the drivers' books. Two other men worked there, but Precious worked much harder. They sat at their tables and talked and drank tea. 'You are working too hard,' they said. 'You are trying to take our jobs.' Precious did not understand. She always worked as hard as she could.

One day she found a mistake of two thousand pula★ in the company's books. She showed the mistake to her cousin's husband. Someone in the company was stealing money. It was one of the men who worked with Precious. The man lost his job. That was the beginning of Mma Ramotswe's detective work.

Precious worked in the bus company office for four years. Every weekend she travelled up to Mochudi on one of the company's buses, and visited her father. She told him about her week in the bus office and he told her about his cattle.

One day, on the way back from Mochudi, she met Note Makoti. Note was wearing a red shirt and he had a proud, handsome face. Next to him on the seat was a music case. When the bus stopped in Gaborone, he got off. This was not her stop, but Precious got off too. Note was standing there, smiling at her.

'I saw you on that bus,' he said. He pointed to the case at his feet. 'I am a musician. I play in the bar at the President Hotel. You can come and listen. I am going there now.'

They walked to the bar and he bought her a drink. She sat at a table at the back. Then he played and she listened. She felt proud that she was his guest. She had a boyfriend now, a musician.

The following Friday, outside the bar and away from the noise of the drinkers, Note Makoti said, 'I want to get married soon. You are a nice girl and you will make a good wife. I will speak to

★ pula: money of Botswana

your father about this. I hope he will not want a lot of cattle for you. But first I must teach you what wives are for.'

He put his arm round her and moved her back in the soft grass. Then he started to kiss her. 'Girls must learn this thing. Has anybody taught you?' he asked.

She shook her head.

'Good,' he said. 'Then I will teach you. Right now.'

He hurt her. When she asked him to stop, he hit her across the face. Then he kissed her. He was sorry, he said. But then he hurt her again and hit her hard with his belt.

Note Makoti visited her father three weeks later and asked him for Precious. Her father did not like Note and he did not want Precious to marry him. But Precious wanted to marry Note. He was not a good man, but perhaps she could change him. And there was something more. She felt that Note's child was deep inside her, like a tiny bird.

After the wedding, Note and Precious lived in Gaborone. Precious went with Note to the bars, and he was kind to her. But he had many friends there who only talked about music. So Precious stopped going to the bars and stayed at home.

One night Note came home late, smelling of beer. He pushed Precious down on the bed and started hitting her with his belt. She cried out, but he was too strong.

'Don't hurt the baby.'

'Baby! Why do you talk about this baby? It is not mine. I am not the father of a baby. I will have to punish you now.'

He hurt her again and she had to go to the hospital. The doctor there gave her medicine for the pain. When she returned home the next day, neither Note nor his music case was there.

Precious went back to Mochudi, to her father. She stayed there, looking after him, for the next fourteen years. When Note's child was born, it lived for only five days. Her father died soon after her thirty-fourth birthday. She never saw Note again.

8

Chapter 3   The Missing Husband

After her father's death, Mma Ramotswe went to see a lawyer.

'There is a lot of money for you from the sale of your father's cattle,' he said. 'You can buy a house, and a business.'

'I am going to buy both of these,' said Mma Ramotswe.

'What sort of business?' asked the lawyer. 'A shop?'

'A detective agency.'

The lawyer looked surprised. 'There are none for sale.'

'I know that,' said Mma Ramotswe. 'I will have to start from the beginning.'

'It's easy to lose money in business,' said the lawyer. 'Can women be detectives? Do you think they can?'

'Why not?' said Mma Ramotswe. 'Women understand what's happening. They are the ones with eyes. Have you heard of Agatha Christie?'

'Agatha Christie?' said the lawyer. 'Of course I know her. Yes, that is true. A woman sees more than a man.'

'So,' said Mma Ramotswe, 'when people see a sign, "No. 1 Ladies' Detective Agency," what will they think? They'll think, "Those ladies will understand what's happening." '

Mma Ramotswe found a house in a road called Zebra Drive. It was a fine house, but it was expensive. Then she looked for a place for the business. That was more difficult, but at last she found a small building near Kgale Hill. It was a good place, because people walked down that road on their way into town.

There was a lot to do. Mma Ramotswe painted the building red on the outside and white on the inside, and then she bought two desks and two chairs. Her friend Mr JLB Matekoni, owner of Tlokweng Road Speedy Cars, brought her an old typewriter that he did not need.

Next she had to find a secretary. She telephoned the Botswana College of Secretarial and Office Skills. They had the perfect woman, they said. Her name was Mma Makutsi and she had the best examination result of 97%. Mma Makutsi was a thin woman with a long face, large glasses and a warm smile. Mma Ramotswe liked her immediately.

They opened the office on a Monday. Mma Ramotswe sat at her desk and Mma Makutsi sat at hers, behind the typewriter. She looked at Mma Ramotswe and smiled.

'I am ready for work,' she said. 'I am ready to start.'

'Mmm,' said Mma Ramotswe. 'We have only just opened. We will have to wait for a client to come.'

Mma Ramotswe was worried. Was the detective agency a terrible mistake? Nobody wanted a private detective and nobody wanted her. She was just Precious Ramotswe from Mochudi.

A chicken came into the room and started to look for food.

'Get out!' shouted Mma Makutsi. 'No chickens in here!'

At ten o'clock Mma Makutsi got up from her desk. She went into the back room to make the tea. At eleven o'clock they had another cup. At twelve o'clock Mma Ramotswe decided to walk down the road to the shops.

She was standing in a shop when Mma Makutsi hurried through the door.

'Mma Ramotswe,' she said. 'There is a client in the office. She has a big problem. A missing man. Come quickly.'

The client was called Mma Malatsi. Mma Makutsi made a cup of strong tea while Mma Malatsi talked to Mma Ramotswe.

'My husband is missing,' she said. 'His name is Peter Malatsi. He's forty and he has − had − has a business selling furniture. It's a good business and he has done well. So he hasn't run away because he has problems with money.'

'You know what men are like,' said Mma Ramotswe carefully. 'Another woman, perhaps? Do you think . . . '

Mma Malatsi shook her head. 'I don't think so,' she said. 'My husband joined a Christian group a year ago. I don't know who

Mma Ramotswe sat at her desk and Mma Makutsi sat at hers.

they are. He was usually with them on a Sunday. In fact, he disappeared on a Sunday. I thought he was at church.'

This was not a difficult problem, thought Mma Ramotswe. Peter Malatsi was with a young Christian woman. She was sure about that. She made a list of five Christian groups and went to see the head of each group. The first three knew nothing about Peter Malatsi. But then she went to see the head of the fourth group, the Reverend Shadreck Mapeli.

'Are you from the police?' asked the Reverend in a worried voice. 'Are you a policeman?'

'Policewoman,' said Mma Ramotswe. 'No. I'm a private detective.'

'Who sent you?'

'Mma Malatsi.'

'Oh!' said the Reverend. 'He had no wife,' he said.'

'Well, he did,' said Mma Ramotswe. 'And she wants to know where he is.'

'He's dead,' said the Reverend sadly.

'You must tell me how it happened,' said Mma Ramotswe.

The Reverend took Mma Ramotswe to the river. It was the rainy season and the water in the river was very high.

'We have our baptisms here,' said the Reverend. 'On that Sunday I was baptising Peter and five other people. They were standing in the water. I was following them, but then I turned round. When I turned back again, Peter wasn't there.'

Mma Ramotswe looked at the water. It was not a big river, but in the rainy season it could be dangerous. But where was Peter Malatsi's body? Suddenly she had a terrible idea.

'You didn't tell the police,' she said to the Reverend. 'Why not?'

The Reverend looked down at the ground. 'If people find out about poor Peter's accident, I will have to go to court,' he said. 'Perhaps I will have to pay a lot of money. Then our Church will not have any money and we will not be able to continue our good work. Do you understand?'

Mma Ramotswe touched the Reverend on the arm. 'I don't think that you acted badly,' she said.

The Reverend smiled. 'Those are kind words, my sister,' he said. 'Thank you.'

Mma Ramotswe drove back home. She had a neighbour with five dogs.

'I need a dog to help me with my work,' said Mma Ramotswe. 'Can I borrow one of yours?'

'I'll give you this dog here,' said the neighbour. 'He's the oldest, and he has a very good nose. He will make a good detective dog.'

Mma Ramotswe took the dog. It was large and yellow and had a bad smell. That night, she put it into her van and drove to the river. She also took her father's gun. She pushed a thick stick into the soft ground near the river and tied the dog to the stick. Then she waited.

Two hours passed. Then suddenly the dog made a noise. It was standing and looking towards the river. Something was coming out of the water. It was a large crocodile.

The crocodile moved slowly towards the frightened dog. Then Mma Ramotswe picked up the gun, pointed it carefully and shot the crocodile. The crocodile gave a big jump into the air, fell and landed on its back in the water. Then it stopped moving.

Mma Ramotswe's hand was shaking as she put the gun down. She did not like to shoot animals. Poor crocodile. No crocodiles usually came to this river. What was it doing there?

She took a knife and cut the crocodile's soft stomach open. Inside there were some pieces of smelly fish. There was also a man's watch.

The next day, Mma Ramotswe visited Mma Malatsi. She explained about the crocodile.

'Did this belong to your husband?' she asked, handing her the watch.

Mma Malatsi took the watch and looked at it. 'Yes,' she said calmly. 'Well, now I know that he is dead – not in the arms of another woman. That's better, isn't it?'

'I think it is,' Mma Ramotswe agreed. 'I had a husband but he made me very unhappy. I am glad that I don't have a husband now. But I'm sorry that you've lost your husband.'

'Yes, it's sad,' said Mma Malatsi. 'But I have lots to do.'

Chapter 4   The Teacher's Letter

Mma Ramotswe was pleased with the success of the No. 1 Ladies' Detective Agency. The first mystery, the mystery of the missing husband, was solved. Mma Makutsi typed a report and also a bill. Then the bill was sent to Mma Malatsi.

It was Mma Makutsi's job to open the letters. But in the first week of the agency, there were very few letters. Then one day in the second week, a letter arrived in a dirty white envelope. Mma Makutsi read it to Mma Ramotswe.

Dear Mma Ramotswe,

I read about your agency in the newspaper. I am very proud for Botswana that we now have a person like you in this country.

I am the teacher at the small school at Katsana Village, fifty kilometres from Gaborone. My wife and I have two daughters and a son of eleven. But two months ago, my son disappeared.

We went to the police. They made a big search and asked questions everywhere. But nobody knew anything about our son. I searched the land around our village but I could not find him. I called and called, but my son never answered me.

He knew many things about the land and he was always very careful.

14

There are no dangerous wild animals near us. How can a boy disappear like this?

I am not a rich man. I have no money to pay a private detective. But I ask you, Mma, to help me in one small way. When you are asking people about other things, please ask them about my son. If you hear anything, please send a note to me, the teacher at Katsana Village.

Ernest Molai Pakotati.

Mma Makutsi stopped reading and looked at Mma Ramotswe.

'Do you know anything about this?' asked Mma Ramotswe. 'Have you heard anything about a missing boy?'

'I think so,' said Mma Makutsi. 'There was something in the newspaper about a search for a boy.'

'I can ask people,' Mma Ramotswe said. 'But I don't think I can do very much for this poor Daddy.'

'No,' said Mma Makutsi. 'We can't help that poor man.'

They sent a letter to the teacher. But when Mma Ramotswe was cooking supper in her house in Zebra Drive that evening, she thought again about the missing boy.

Where could the boy be? Perhaps he was in danger somewhere. It was terrible for the teacher and his wife. Was the child stolen by a stranger? How could anyone do that to a young child? How could these bad things happen in Botswana?

'Perhaps I should not be a detective,' she thought. 'I want to help people. But sometimes their problems make me too sad.'

The next day, Mma Ramotswe went to see her friend, Mr JLB Matekoni. Mr JLB Matekoni was forty-five, ten years older than Mma Ramotswe, and came from the same village, Mochudi. He was very good at repairing cars. His business, Tlokweng Road Speedy Cars, was very successful.

Mr JLB Matekoni was not handsome, but he had a very kind face. Mma Ramotswe liked to go to his garage to drink tea. They always talked about local news. Today they talked about the problems of owning a business. Mma Ramotswe was worried because the No. 1 Ladies' Detective Agency was not making enough money.

'Your secretary — the one with the big glasses,' said Mr JLB Matekoni. 'She is costing you a lot of money.'

'I know,' said Mma Ramotswe. 'But you need a secretary if you have an office.'

'Then you need to get better clients,' said Mr JLB Matekoni. 'You need somebody rich to bring you a problem. Rich men have their troubles too.'

'I had a letter last week,' said Mma Ramotswe. 'It made me very sad because I couldn't help the man.' She told Mr JLB Matekoni about the teacher's letter.

'I read about that missing boy in the newspaper,' he said. 'But it is useless to search for him.'

'Why?' asked Mma Ramotswe.

Mr JLB Matekoni was silent. 'Because that boy is dead,' he said at last. 'No animal took him.'

Mma Ramotswe was silent too, thinking of the teacher. She was remembering the time when her own child died. It was like the end of your world. The stars went out and the moon disappeared. The birds became silent.

'Why do you say that he is dead?' she asked. 'Perhaps he is lost.'

'No,' said Mr JLB Matekoni. 'A witchdoctor has taken him.'

Mma Ramotswe put her cup down on the table. 'How can you be sure?'

'You know what happens, Mma Ramotswe,' said Mr JLB Matekoni. 'We Africans don't like to talk about it, do we? It is a subject that brings fear to our hearts. We know what happens to missing children. We know.'

Mma Ramotswe looked up at him. Mr JLB Matekoni was probably right. A witchdoctor took the boy and killed him. Then

16

his body was used for medicine – *muti* – for a rich man. It was terrible that these things still happened in modern Botswana.

'You may be right,' she said. 'That poor boy . . .'

'Of course I'm right,' said Mr JLB Matekoni. 'And why do you think that poor man had to write that letter to you? The police are doing nothing to find out about the boy. They are afraid. We are all afraid – maybe even you.'

Chapter 5   The Boyfriend

One morning, Mma Ramotswe received a telephone call from Mr Paliwalar Patel, one of the richest men in Botswana.

Mr Patel was from an Indian family. When he was twenty-five, he came to Botswana. He bought a shop. Now he owned eight shops and a hotel. Mr Patel's youngest daughter, Nandira, was sixteen. She went to the Maru-a-Pula School in Gaborone, the best and most expensive private school in Botswana.

Mr Patel asked Mma Ramotswe to come and see him at home that evening. She was very pleased and excited. Before she went out, she telephoned Mr JLB Matekoni.

'You told me to get a rich client. And now I have. Mr Patel.'

'He is a very rich man,' said Mr JLB Matekoni. 'He has four Mercedes Benzes. Four!'

That evening, Mma Ramotswe drove to Mr Patel's big house in her tiny white van. When she met her client, she was very surprised. Mma Ramotswe was not tall, but Mr Patel was even smaller than she was.

He took her into his private office.

'Sit down, please,' said Mr Patel, pointing to a comfortable armchair. 'I am a man with a happy family. But I am worried about my youngest child, my little Nandira. She is doing well at school, but . . . You know about young people, don't you? You know how young people are in these modern days?'

'Yes,' said Mma Ramotswe. 'They often bring a lot of worry to their parents.'

'That's what is worrying me,' said Mr Patel angrily. 'That's what is happening. And I will not accept that. Not in my family.'

'Accept what?' asked Mma Ramotswe.

'Boys,' said Mr Patel. 'My Nandira is seeing a boy in secret. She says it is not true. But I know that there is a boy. And this is not acceptable in this family – in this house. I want you to find out about this boy, and then I will speak to him.'

'Why don't you ask Nandira about the young man?' asked Mma Ramotswe.

'I have asked her for three or four weeks,' said Mr Patel. 'But she gives no answer.'

Mma Ramotswe looked down at her feet. She felt sorry for Mr Patel's daughter. Her father wanted to protect her too much.

'I'll find out for you,' she said at last. 'But I don't like the idea of watching a child. They must have their own lives.'

'No!' shouted Mr Patel. 'My father still hit me when I was twenty-two!'

'I am a modern lady,' said Mma Ramotswe. 'So perhaps we have different ideas. But I have agreed to do as you have asked. Please show me a photograph of Nandira, so I will know her.'

'No need,' said Mr Patel. 'You can meet her.'

'But then she will know me,' said Mma Ramotswe. 'I won't be able to follow her in secret.'

'Ah!' said Mr Patel. 'You are right. You detectives are very clever men.'

'Women,' said Mma Ramotswe.

The next afternoon, Mma Ramotswe waited outside Nandira's expensive private school. At twenty past three, Nandira came out of the school entrance, carrying her bag. Mma Ramotswe waited for a few minutes, and then followed her slowly. At the end of the road, Nandira turned the corner.

Mma Ramotswe followed Nandira round the corner. The road was empty. It was a quiet road with only three houses on each side.

'Has Nandira gone into one of those houses?' thought Mma Ramotswe. 'Does her boyfriend live there?'

That evening, Mr Patel telephoned her. 'Do you have any information to report to me yet?' he asked.

'No,' said Mma Ramotswe. 'But I hope I will be more successful tomorrow.'

'Not very good,' said Mr Patel. 'Not very good. Well, I have something to report to you. Nandira came home three hours after school finished – three hours. Then this evening my wife found a note on the table. It said, "See you tomorrow, Jack." Now who is this Jack? Who is this person? Is that a girl's name?'

'No,' said Mma Ramotswe. 'It sounds like a boy.'

'Exactly!' said Mr Patel. 'That is the boy, I think. Jack who? Where does he live? You must find out and tell me everything.'

The next afternoon, Mma Ramotswe waited again outside the school. At last Nandira came out with a friend and the two girls got into a blue car. The car drove away and Mma Ramotswe followed it in her tiny white van.

The blue car drove to the main shopping centre and parked outside the President Hotel. Mma Ramotswe parked the tiny white van too. She watched the two girls get out with an older woman.

'She's the mother of Nandira's friend,' thought Mma Ramotswe.

The girls looked in the window of a shoe shop. Then they walked up to the Botswana Book Centre and went inside.

Mma Ramotswe followed them. The Book Centre was a popular meeting place for young people, but today there were very few customers inside. The girls were at the other end of the shop, looking at a shelf of language books. They were talking and laughing. Were they waiting for someone?

Mma Ramotswe reached for a book. It was called *Snakes of Botswana* and it had very good pictures. Mma Ramotswe started reading about dangerous snakes. Suddenly she remembered the girls. She looked up quickly, but they were not there!

She put the book back on the shelf and ran out into the square, but she could not see the girls anywhere. She ran back to the President Hotel and saw the blue car leaving. But only the mother was inside.

There was a shop with a woman selling dresses.

'Did you see two girls come out of the Book Centre?' asked Mma Ramotswe. 'One Indian girl and one African?'

'I saw them,' said the woman. 'They went over to the cinema. They went inside, then they came out and went away.'

'Thank you,' said Mma Ramotswe, pressing a ten-pula note into the woman's hand.

She walked over to the cinema and looked at the times of the films. There was a film that evening.

When Mma Ramotswe got home, Mr Patel telephoned.

'My daughter says she is going out,' he said. 'She is going to see a friend about some homework. But I know she is lying.'

'Yes,' said Mma Ramotswe. 'I'm afraid she is. But I know where she's going. I shall be there. Don't worry.'

'She is going to see this Jack?' shouted Mr Patel.

'Probably,' said Mma Ramotswe. 'But I will give you a report tomorrow.'

There were very few people in the cinema when Mma Ramotswe arrived. She sat in a seat at the back, waiting for Nandira and Jack. Nandira arrived five minutes before the film. She was alone. She stood in the doorway, looking round. Then she walked across to Mma Ramotswe and sat down in the seat next to her.

Mma Ramotswe started reading about dangerous snakes.

'Good evening, Mma,' she said politely. 'I saw you this afternoon. I saw you outside my school. Then I saw you in the Book Centre. Then you asked the woman in the dress shop about me. She told me. So why are you following me?'

Mma Ramotswe thought quickly. She decided to be honest with Nandira, so she told her about her father.

'He wants to find out if you are seeing boys,' she said. 'He's worried about it.' Nandira looked pleased. 'And are you?' asked Mma Ramotswe. 'Are you going out with lots of boys?'

'No,' said Nandira quietly. 'Not really.'

'But this Jack?' asked Mma Ramotswe. 'Who is he?'

'Jack doesn't exist,' said Nandira. 'I want them − my family − to think I've got a boyfriend. Somebody I chose. Not somebody they chose for me. Do you understand that?'

'Yes,' said Mma Ramotswe, putting a hand on Nandira's arm. 'I understand.'

'It's been a silly game, I know,' Nandira said. 'You will tell my father that Jack isn't real. Then perhaps he will leave me to live my own life.'

'I don't know if he will listen to me,' said Mma Ramotswe. 'But I will try and talk to him.'

They watched the film together, and both enjoyed it. Then Mma Ramotswe drove Nandira home in her tiny white van.

Mma Ramotswe went to see Mr Patel early the next morning.

'You've got bad news for me,' he said. 'What is it? I am very worried. You will not understand a father's worries.'

Mma Ramotswe smiled. 'The news is good,' she said. 'There is no boyfriend. Jack is not real. Nandira imagined a boyfriend because she wants to be freer. Give her time for her own life. Don't ask her questions all the time.'

Mr Patel closed his eyes and thought. 'Why should I do this?' he said. 'Why should I accept these modern ideas?'

22

'Because if you don't,' said Mma Ramotswe, 'she will look for a real boyfriend.'

Mr Patel stood up. 'You are a very clever woman,' he said. 'And I'm going to do as you suggest. I will leave her to live her life. And in two or three years I am sure that I can help her find a good husband.'

'Yes,' said Mma Ramotswe. 'You probably can.'

♦

Mma Ramotswe often thought about Nandira when she drove past Mr Patel's house. But she did not see Nandira again until nearly a year later. She was having coffee one Saturday morning at the President Hotel when someone touched her on the shoulder. She turned round, and there was Nandira with a young man. He was about eighteen with a pleasant, open face.

'Mma Ramotswe,' said Nandira in a friendly way. 'This is my friend. I don't think you have met him.'

The young man smiled and held out his hand. 'Jack,' he said.

Chapter 6   The Stolen Car

Mma Ramotswe sent a bill for two thousand pula to Mr Patel and he paid it immediately. Mma Ramotswe was very pleased because this was a lot of money.

Three days later, another client came to see Mma Ramotswe. She was called Mma Pekwane, and she seemed very nervous.

'I'm worried that my husband has done a terrible thing,' she said.

'Many men do terrible things,' said Mma Ramotswe kindly. 'All wives are worried about their husbands. You are not alone.'

'But this thing is very terrible,' said Mma Pekwane. 'He has a stolen car.'

'Are you sure that it is stolen?' asked Mma Ramotswe. 'Did he tell you that?'

'A man gave it to him, he said,' replied Mma Pekwane. 'This man had two Mercedes Benzes and only needed one.'

Mma Ramotswe laughed. 'How can men believe that we are so stupid?' She looked at Mma Pekwane. 'Do you want me to tell you what to do?' she asked. 'Is that what you want?'

'No,' said Mma Pekwane. 'I don't want that. I have decided what I want to do. I want to give the car back to its owner.'

'You want to go to the police?' asked Mma Ramotswe. 'You want to tell them that your husband is a thief?'

'No, I don't want that. I want to give the car back to its owner without telling the police. Then they won't find out that my husband stole this car.'

'But why have you come to me about this?' asked Mma Ramotswe. 'How can I help?'

'I want you to find out who owns that car,' said Mma Pekwane. 'Then I want you to steal it from my husband and give it back to its owner. That's all.'

That evening, Mma Ramotswe telephoned Mr JLB Matekoni.

'Where do stolen Mercedes Benzes come from?' she asked.

'From over the border in South Africa,' said Mr JLB Matekoni. 'They are stolen in South Africa and brought to Botswana. They are painted with a different colour and their number plates are changed. Then they are sold cheaply or sent up to Zambia.'

'How can you find out if a car is stolen?' asked Mma Ramotswe.

'There's usually another number somewhere on the car,' said Mr JLB Matekoni. 'You have to know where to look for this number. You have to know what you're doing.'

'*You* know what you're doing,' said Mma Ramotswe. 'Can you help me?'

Mr JLB Matekoni did not like stolen cars. But Mma Ramotswe needed his help and so there was only one answer.

'Tell me where and when,' he said.

The next evening, Mma Ramotswe and Mr JLB Matekoni went into Mma Pekwane's garden. The Mercedes Benz was parked outside the house. Mr JLB Matekoni got down under the car, shone a light up into it and found the number.

'Are you sure that's enough?' asked Mma Ramotswe. 'Will they know from that number if this car is stolen?'

'Yes,' said Mr JLB Matekoni. 'They will know.'

Mma Ramotswe had an old school friend called Billy Pilani. Now Billy was a police chief in South Africa. That weekend, Mma Ramotswe drove her tiny white van over the border to Mafikeng to see him. They met at the Railway Café, and she bought him a cup of coffee. Then she gave him a piece of paper with the number from the car on it.

'I want you to find out who owns this car,' she said. 'Then I want you to tell the owner, or the owner's insurance company, to come up to Gaborone. They will find the car in an agreed place. They must bring the car's South African number plates. Then they can drive it home.'

Billy Pilani looked surprised. 'Isn't there any money to pay?' he asked.

'No,' said Mma Ramotswe. 'We just have to get the car back to its owner. That's all.'

Billy Pilani telephoned Mma Ramotswe the next day.

'I have found that car on our list of stolen cars,' he said. 'The owner's insurance company are very happy to get it back. They will send one of their men to pick it up.'

'Good,' said Mma Ramotswe. 'The car will be outside the African Shopping Centre in Gaborone next Tuesday morning at seven o'clock. The man must come there with the number plates.'

25

Everything was agreed. At five o'clock on Tuesday morning, Mma Ramotswe went to the Pekwane house. She found the keys of the car on the ground outside the bedroom window.

'Good,' she thought. 'Mma Pekwane has done as I asked.'

Mma Ramotswe started the car and drove it away. Mma Pekwane's husband did not hear her. He did not notice that his Mercedes Benz was missing until almost eight o'clock.

'Call the police!' shouted Mma Pekwane. 'Quick!'

'Maybe later,' said her husband slowly. 'First, I think *I* shall look for it.'

'So I was right,' thought Mma Pekwane. 'He knows he can't go to the police about this car. The police will ask him a lot of questions. They will find out that the car is stolen.'

She saw Mma Ramotswe later that day and thanked her.

'I feel much better,' she said. 'I will be able to sleep at night without worrying about my husband.'

'I'm very pleased,' said Mma Ramotswe. 'And maybe your husband has learned a lesson too.'

◆

Mma Ramotswe was very happy with her detective agency and her lovely house in Zebra Drive. She enjoyed her life and had many friends. Her best friend was Mr JLB Matekoni. One day, at his garage, they started talking about the past.

'I have made hundreds of mistakes in my life . . .' said Mr JLB Matekoni, pouring tea into Mma Ramotswe's cup. 'I didn't know then what I know now.'

Mma Ramotswe looked at him in surprise. 'You have your business, money in the bank, your own house,' she said. 'I can't see what mistakes you have made. Not like me.'

'But you are too clever to make mistakes,' said Mr JLB Matekoni.

'I married Note.'

Mr JLB Matekoni thought. 'Yes,' he said. 'That was a bad mistake.' They were silent, then Mr JLB Matekoni stood up. 'I would like you to marry me,' he said. 'That will not be a mistake.'

Mma Ramotswe hid her surprise. She smiled at her friend.

'You are a good, kind man,' she said. 'You are like my Daddy . . . a bit. But I cannot get married again. Ever. I am happy as I am. I have got the agency, and the house. My life is full.'

Mr JLB Matekoni sat down. He looked very sad. Mma Ramotswe reached out to touch him. But he moved away, as a burned man moves away from a fire.

'I am very sorry,' she said. 'But I don't want to marry anybody.'

Mr JLB Matekoni took her cup and poured her more tea. He was silent now. He was not angry, but he had no more words.

Chapter 7   A Missing Finger

Mma Ramotswe knew the owner of one of the factories in Gaborone. Hector Lepodise asked Mma Ramotswe to meet him for coffee at the President Hotel.

'I have a problem,' he said. 'One of my workers, Solomon Moretsi, left his job suddenly. A few weeks later, I had a letter from his lawyer up in Mahalapye. He is asking me to pay Moretsi four thousand pula. He says Moretsi lost a finger in an accident in my factory.'

'And was there an accident?' asked Mma Ramotswe.

'There is an accident book in the factory,' said Hector. 'If anyone gets hurt, they must write it down in the book. I looked in the book. There was an accident some days before Moretsi left. But it was only a cut.'

Mma Ramotswe went to the factory with Hector and looked in the book. She read the information about Moretsi's accident:

MORETSI CUT HIS FINGER. NO. 2 FINGER
COUNTING FROM THUMB. MACHINE DID IT.
RIGHT HAND. SIGNED: SOLOMON MORETSI.

Then she read the letter from Moretsi's lawyer.

My client had an accident at your factory on 10th May. He went to the Princess Marina Hospital the next day. But the finger went bad. So the following week it was cut off (see hospital report).

The accident happened because the machines in your factory are not safe. So you must pay my client four thousand pula, or he will go to a judge. Then you will have to pay more money.

Mma Ramotswe read the hospital report. It had the right date, the paper looked real and there was the signature of a doctor.

'So he cut his finger and it went bad,' she said. 'What does your insurance company say?'

'They have agreed to pay Moretsi four thousand pula,' said Hector. 'But I don't want to pay this man. I never liked him. And some of the other workers didn't like him either. I don't believe his story about losing a finger in my factory.'

'But a man with a missing finger needs money,' said Mma Ramotswe. 'Why don't you just pay him?'

'Because if I pay him this time, perhaps he will do the same thing again,' said Hector. 'I don't think he is an honest man. But if I am wrong, then I will pay him.'

'Is Moretsi lying?' thought Mma Ramotswe. 'Did he lose his finger after the accident in Hector's factory or not?'

That night she did not sleep well. It was very hot, and the dogs in the town were making a lot of noise. She got up and made herself some tea, and thought about Moretsi. Then she had an idea.

'Perhaps Moretsi has received money from an insurance company before,' she thought.

There were six large insurance companies in Gaborone. Next morning, Mma Ramotswe telephoned them. The first three could not help her, but the fourth, the Kalahari Accident Insurance Company, had some interesting information.

'We had a claim about a man called Moretsi three years ago,' said a woman from the company. 'It was from a garage in town. One of their workers lost a finger in an accident. The garage was insured with us, so we had to pay.'

Mma Ramotswe felt very excited. 'Four thousand pula?'

'Nearly. Three thousand eight hundred.'

'Right hand?' asked Mma Ramotswe. 'Second finger counting from the thumb?'

'There's a hospital report,' said the woman. 'Yes, that's right. The finger went bad, so it was cut off.'

Mma Ramotswe put down the phone, feeling very pleased. So Moretsi lost a finger before he started work in Hector's factory.

Mma Ramotswe decided to drive to Mahalapye. It was a two-hour drive on a bad road, but she was happy to go there. She wanted to meet Moretsi and his lawyer.

Mma Ramotswe left Mma Makutsi in the office and drove up to Mahalapye in the tiny white van. It was a very hot day. She drove past the hills to the east of Mochudi and into the wide valley. All around there was nothing – just flat, empty country.

Suddenly a big green snake moved quickly across the road. Mma Ramotswe could not stop the van in time. She slowed down, looking behind her in the mirror. But she could not see the snake in the road. Where was it?

She stopped the van, but she still could not see the snake. Perhaps it was somewhere in the van. Sometimes drivers picked up snakes without knowing. They did not see the snake in their car. Then the snake bit them. They died as they were driving.

Mma Ramotswe got out of the tiny white van and stood next to it. Was the snake in the van? How could she get it out?

The road was very quiet, but then she saw a car. As it came nearer, it slowed down.

'Are you in trouble, Mma?' the driver called out politely.

Mma Ramotswe crossed the road and explained about the snake. The man turned off his engine and got out of the car.

'Snakes can get into the engine,' he said. 'It can be dangerous. You were right to stop.' He went over to the van and looked inside the engine. 'Don't move,' he said very softly. 'There it is.'

Mma Ramotswe looked inside. At first she could not see anything unusual. Then suddenly the snake moved a little and she saw it.

'Walk very carefully back to the door,' said the man. 'Get into the van and start the engine. Understand?'

Mma Ramotswe did as she was told. The engine started immediately. There was a noise from the front. After some time, the man told her to switch the engine off.

'You can come out,' he called. 'That's the end of the snake!'

Mma Ramotswe got out of the van and walked round to the front. She looked into the engine and saw the snake. It was cut into two pieces.

'You are safe now,' said the man.

Mma Ramotswe thanked him and drove off. This journey to Mahalapye was becoming an adventure.

When she got to Mahalapye, she went to the lawyer's office.

'My client, Mr Moretsi, is going to be a little late,' said the lawyer.

Mma Ramotswe looked round the office. The room looked poor, with very little furniture.

'So business is not so good these days,' she said.

'It's not bad,' said the lawyer angrily. 'In fact, I am very busy.'

'It probably takes a lot of time,' said Mma Ramotswe, 'listening to your clients' lies.'

'My clients do not lie,' said the lawyer slowly.

'Oh no?' said Mma Ramotswe. 'What about Mr Moretsi? How many fingers has he got?'

'Don't move,' he said very softly. 'There it is.'

'Nine,' said the lawyer. 'Or nine and a half. You know that.'

'Very interesting,' said Mma Ramotswe. 'So how did he make a successful claim to Kalahari Accident Insurance Company three years ago? It was for a finger lost in an accident in a garage.'

'Three years ago?' said the lawyer in a weak voice. 'A finger?'

'Yes,' said Mma Ramotswe. 'He asked for four thousand pula. The insurance company paid him three thousand eight hundred. The company gave me the claim number, if you want to check.'

The lawyer said nothing, and Mma Ramotswe felt sorry for him. He was just trying to do his job.

'Show me the report from the hospital,' she said. The lawyer took out a report from his desk, and Mma Ramotswe looked at it. 'Look,' she said. 'It's just as I thought. Look at the date there. Someone has changed it. Mr Moretsi's finger was cut off once, perhaps as the result of an accident. But the date has changed. So now it looks like a new accident.'

The lawyer took the paper and held it up to the light. You could see the change in the date clearly.

Just then, Moretsi arrived.

'Sit down,' said the lawyer coldly.

Moretsi looked surprised. But he did as he was told.

'So you're the lady who is going to pay . . .' he began.

'She has not come to pay anything,' said the lawyer. 'She has come to ask you a question. Why do you claim for lost fingers all the time?'

'Yes,' said Mma Ramotswe. 'You claim, I believe, that you lost three fingers. But if I look at your hand, I see only one missing finger. This is wonderful! Perhaps you know a drug that grows new fingers!'

'*Three* fingers?' asked the lawyer in surprise.

'Yes,' said Mma Ramotswe. 'There was the Kalahari Accident Insurance Company. And then there was . . . What was the name of the other company? I've forgotten.'

'Star Insurance,' said Moretsi quietly.

'Ah!' said Mma Ramotswe. 'Thank you for that.'

The lawyer waved the hospital report at Moretsi.

'That is the end of your game,' he said angrily.

'Why did you do it?' asked Mma Ramotswe. 'Just tell me.'

'I am looking after my parents,' said Moretsi. 'And I have a sister who is sick with a terrible illness. The illness that is killing everybody these days. I have to look after her children.'

Mma Ramotswe looked into his eyes. Moretsi was not lying.

'If Moretsi goes to prison, his parents and sister will suffer more,' she thought. 'All right,' she said. 'I will not tell the police about this. But you must promise that there will be no more lost fingers. Do you understand?'

'Yes,' said Moretsi quickly. 'You are a good lady.'

'But sometimes I can be a very unpleasant lady,' said Mma Ramotswe, looking at the lawyer. 'Some people in this country, some men, think that women are soft. Well, I'm not. I killed a big snake on the way here today.'

'Oh?' said the lawyer. 'What did you do?'

'I cut it into two pieces,' said Mma Ramotswe. 'Two pieces.'

Chapter 8   The Bone

Mma Ramotswe did not want Mr JLB Matekoni as a husband, but she liked him very much as a friend. He was her best friend in Gaborone, and she did not want to lose him.

A few days later, she went to see him. But Mr JLB Matekoni was very quiet and did not say very much. He did not seem to be listening, and was looking out of the window.

'Perhaps he is angry because I didn't want to marry him,' thought Mma Ramotswe. 'Are you worried about something?' she asked. 'What are you thinking about?'

Mr JLB Matekoni stood up and closed the door. 'I have found something,' he said. 'There was an accident. It was not a bad one. Nobody was hurt. A lorry hit a car and pushed it off the road.'

Mr JLB Matekoni sat down and looked at his hands.

'And?' said Mma Ramotswe.

'I brought the car to my garage for repair. I'll show it to you later. I checked everything in the car. When I was checking the electric parts, I opened the box in front of the passenger seat. And I found something inside. A little bag.' He took out a small bag and put it on the table. The bag was made of animal skin. 'I'll open it,' he said. 'I don't want you to touch it.'

He opened the bag and took out three small things. There was a strange smell coming from them. Now Mma Ramotswe understood. Mr JLB Matekoni did not have to say anything more. The things were *muti* – the medicine of a witchdoctor.

She said nothing as the things were placed on the table. There was a small bone, a piece of skin and a wooden bottle. Mr JLB Matekoni touched the things with a pencil.

'See,' he said. 'I found these things.'

Mma Ramotswe got up and walked towards the door. She felt sick. Then the feeling passed and she turned round.

'I'm going to take that bone and check it,' she said. 'Perhaps it is from an animal.'

Mr JLB Matekoni shook his head. 'It won't be,' he said. 'I know what they'll say.'

'Put it in an envelope and I'll take it,' said Mma Ramotswe.

Mr JLB Matekoni opened his mouth to speak. 'These things are dangerous,' he wanted to say. But then he closed his mouth again. He did not believe in witchdoctors' medicine. Or did he?

'There's one thing that I would like to know,' said Mma Ramotswe as she left the office. 'That car – who owned it?'

Mr JLB Matekoni kept his voice low while he told her. 'Charlie Gotso,' he said. 'Him. That one.'

Mma Ramotswe opened her eyes wide in surprise. 'Gotso?'

Everyone knew Charlie Gotso. He was one of the most important men in Botswana. You always did what he asked. If you did not, life could become very difficult for you.

'Oh,' said Mma Ramotswe.

'Exactly,' said Mr JLB Matekoni.

Mma Ramotswe put the envelope with the bone in her desk. She left it there for a few days, but she could not forget about it. She did not want Mma Makutsi to see it. It was too dangerous. So she took the bone out of her desk and left the office.

'I'm going to the bank,' she told Mma Makutsi.

But Mma Ramotswe did not go to the bank. She drove to the Princess Marina Hospital. She had a friend there, Dr Gulubane.

Dr Gulubane was very pleased to see her. 'Come with me to my office,' he said. 'We can talk there.'

Mma Ramotswe followed him to his small office.

'As you know,' she began, 'I'm a private detective these days. Can you tell me where this bone came from?'

She took out the envelope and opened it. The small bone fell out and Dr Gulubane picked it up.

'It's from a child,' he said. 'Eight or nine years old. Where did you get it?'

Mma Ramotswe could hear the sound of her own heart. 'Somebody showed it to me,' she said. 'But can you tell me anything more? Do you know when . . . when the child died?'

Dr Gulubane looked at the bone again.

'Not long ago,' he said. 'Maybe a few months, maybe less. You can't be sure. But how do you know that the child is dead? People can lose a finger and still live!'

That evening, Mma Ramotswe invited Mr JLB Matekoni to dinner. She told him about her conversation with Dr Gulubane.

'A child?' said Mr JLB Matekoni sadly.

'Yes,' said Mma Ramotswe. 'What do we do?'

Mr JLB Matekoni thought for a time. He did not want any trouble with a man like Charlie Gotso.

'We can go to the police,' he said at last. 'But then Charlie Gotso will hear that I found the bag in his car.'

'I don't think we can go to the police,' said Mma Ramotswe. 'But we can't just forget about this child. I have a plan. Charlie Gotso's car is still in your garage. First you must break the window of the car. Then telephone Charlie Gotso. Tell him thieves broke into his car. Tell him you will pay for a new window. Then wait and see.'

'To see what?'

'Perhaps he will tell you that something is missing from the car. Tell him that you know a lady private detective. Tell him she can help him. That's me, of course.'

'And then?'

'Then I'll take the bag back to him and get the name of the witchdoctor from him. Then we'll think what to do next.'

Mma Ramotswe's plan sounded very simple. So the next morning Mr JLB Matekoni did as Mma Ramotswe asked. He broke a window of Charlie Gotso's car and telephoned Charlie Gotso. In the afternoon, a visitor arrived at his garage. He was dressed like a soldier and wore an expensive snakeskin belt.

'Mr Gotso sent me,' he said. 'He is very angry that someone has broken into his car in your garage.'

'I'm very sorry, Rra,'★ said Mr JLB Matekoni nervously.

'All right, all right,' said the man. 'Just show me the car.'

Mr JLB Matekoni took the man to the car. The man opened the door and looked inside. Then he opened the box in front of the passenger seat.

'There is something missing from here,' he said. 'Do you know

★ Rra: Sir or Mr in Setswana, the language that most people in Botswana speak

36

'There is something missing from here.'

anything about that?' Mr JLB Matekoni shook his head. 'Mr Gotso will not be pleased about this,' said the man.

'I know someone who can help,' said Mr JLB Matekoni. 'There's a lady detective. She has an office near Kgale Hill.' Mr JLB Matekoni smiled. 'She's a wonderful lady! She knows about everything that's happening. If I ask her, she'll be able to find out about this thing. She'll find out what happened to it. Perhaps she can even get it back. What is it, this thing?'

'Something that belongs to Mr Gotso,' replied the man. 'Can you ask that lady? Ask her to get this thing back to Mr Gotso.'

'I will ask,' said Mr JLB Matekoni. 'I am sure that she can help.' But Mr JLB Matekoni did not feel happy. 'This is dangerous, and not my business,' he thought. 'I will tell Mma Ramotswe that I repair cars. I cannot repair people's lives.'

He went to the No. 1 Ladies' Detective Agency.

'Well?' asked Mma Ramotswe. 'Did everything go as we planned?'

'Mma Ramotswe, I really think . . .'

'Did Charlie Gotso come round, or did he send one of his men?'

'One of his men. But listen, I am just . . .'

'And did you tell him about me? Did he seem interested?'

'I repair machines. I cannot . . . You see, I have never lied. I have never lied before, even when I was a small boy.'

'You have done very well this time,' said Mma Ramotswe. 'Lies are all right if you are lying for a good reason. And the search for a child's murderer is a very good reason. Are lies worse than murder, Mr JLB Matekoni? Do you think that?'

'Murder is worse. But . . .'

'You didn't think about it carefully, did you? Now you know.'

She looked at him and smiled, and he thought, 'I am lucky. Here is somebody who likes me. Somebody who smiles at me. And she's right. Murder is worse than lies.'

'Come in for tea,' said Mma Ramotswe. 'We must decide what to do next.'

The next day, Mma Ramotswe went to see Charlie Gotso. Charlie Gotso liked fat women and he looked at her with interest.

'You are the woman from Matekoni?'

'Mr JLB Matekoni asked me to help him, Rra. I am a private detective.'

Mr Gotso smiled. 'I have seen your sign. A private detective agency for ladies, or something like that.'

'Not just for ladies, Rra,' said Mma Ramotswe. 'We are lady detectives, but we work for men too. Mr Patel, for example.'

Mr Gotso smiled again. 'You think you can tell men things?'

Mma Ramotswe answered calmly. 'Sometimes. But some men are too proud to listen. We can't tell that sort of man anything.'

Mr Gotso narrowed his eyes. What did she mean? Was she talking about him, or other men?

'You know I lost something from my car,' he said. 'Do you know who took it? Can you get it back for me?'

'I have done that,' said Mma Ramotswe. 'I found out who broke into your car. They were only boys. They gave the thing to me.'

'Where is it?' asked Mr Gotso.

Mma Ramotswe reached into her handbag and took out the small bag. She put it on the table. Mr Gotso reached across and took it.

'This is not mine, of course. I was looking after it for one of my men. I have no idea what it is.'

'*Muti*, Rra. A witchdoctor's medicine. I think it is very expensive and very strong. I would like some medicine like that. But I do not know where I can find it.'

Mr Gotso moved a little. 'Maybe I can help you, Mma.'

Mma Ramotswe thought quickly, and then gave her answer.

39

'I would like you to help me. Then maybe I can help you in some way.'

'In what way can you help me?'

'I think you are a man who likes information. And I hear some very interesting things in my business. For example, I can tell you about that man who is trying to build a shop next to yours in the Shopping Centre. He did some bad things before he came to Gaborone. He wouldn't like people to know, I think.'

'You are a very interesting woman, Mma Ramotswe,' said Mr Gotso. 'I think I understand you very well. I will give you the name of the witchdoctor if you give me this useful information.' He picked up a small piece of paper. 'I'm going to draw you a map. This witchdoctor lives out in the country, not far from Molepolole.'

Chapter 9   The Careless Doctor

Mma Ramotswe had the information now to find a murderer. But there was another mystery to solve. One of Mma Ramotswe's friends, Dr Maketsi, was a doctor at the Princess Marina Hospital. One evening he called into her office on his way home from work.

'I am worried about one of our young doctors, Dr Komoti,' he said. 'He came here about six months ago. At first everything was fine. But then he started making mistakes. Some days his work is very good, but the next day he makes a bad mistake.'

'Are you sure that he is really a doctor?' asked Mma Ramotswe.

'Oh yes,' said Dr Maketsi. 'Before he came to Botswana, he worked in a hospital in Nairobi. I telephoned that hospital. His work was very good, they said. They even sent me a photograph of him. I'm sure that it is the same man.'

'Can't you just test him?' said Mma Ramotswe. 'You could ask him some difficult questions.'

'I've done that,' said Dr Maketsi. 'The first time, he gave very good answers. But the second time, he didn't know how to answer my questions. I'm afraid that he is taking drugs.'

'I'm not sure that I can help,' said Mma Ramotswe. 'Drugs are a business for the police. What do you want me to do?'

'Find out about him,' said Dr Maketsi. 'Follow him. If he is taking drugs, it will be a big problem for the hospital.'

Dr Maketsi gave Mma Ramotswe Dr Komoti's address, his photograph and the number of his car number plate. She started following him two days later. She sat outside the hospital in her tiny white van and waited for him in the evenings. But Dr Komoti always went straight home and stayed there.

Then on Friday afternoon, things changed. Dr Komoti came out of the hospital and got into his car. But this time he did not go home. He turned towards the Lobatse Road. 'This is interesting,' thought Mma Ramotswe. Lobatse was close to the border with South Africa. Was Dr Komoti passing drugs into South Africa, or picking them up from there?

But Dr Komoti did not stop in Lobatse. Mma Ramotswe was worried. Was he going to Mafikeng, in South Africa?

Mma Ramotswe watched Dr Komoti drive across the border. She could not follow him because she did not have her passport. So she went back to Gaborone, feeling angry with herself. Dr Komoti was in South Africa and she had to stay in Botswana.

The next day, Mma Ramotswe went into town and had a cup of coffee with a friend at the President Hotel. As she was walking down the front steps, she saw Dr Komoti.

Mma Ramotswe was very surprised. 'He went to South Africa only yesterday evening,' she thought. 'Why did he come back to Botswana so soon?'

The next Friday, Dr Komoti drove to South Africa again. This time Mma Ramotswe followed him across the border.

In Mafikeng, Dr Komoti stopped outside a house with a large garden and went into one of the houses. Mma Ramotswe drove past and parked the van under a tree. Then she walked back to the house. She pushed the garden gate open carefully and went into the garden. It was very large and untidy.

Suddenly a window at the back of the house opened, and a man looked out. It was Dr Komoti.

'You! Yes, you, fat lady! What are you doing in our garden?'

'It is hot,' Mma Ramotswe called out. 'Can you give me a drink of water?'

The window closed, and a few minutes later the kitchen door opened. Dr Komoti stood on the step, holding a cup of water. He gave it to Mma Ramotswe. She drank the water gratefully.

'What do you want?' he said. 'Are you looking for work?'

Suddenly another man came behind Dr Komoti, and looked over his shoulder. It was another Dr Komoti.

'What does this woman want?' said the second Dr Komoti.

'I was looking at this house,' said Mma Ramotswe. 'I lived here when I was a child. My mother worked in this house as a cook and my father kept the garden tidy. It was better then.'

'We have no time to look after the garden,' said one of the Dr Komotis. 'We are busy men. We are both doctors, you see.'

'Ah!' said Mma Ramotswe. 'Here at the hospital?'

'No,' said the first Dr Komoti. 'I work down near the railway station. My brother . . .'

'I work up that way,' said the other Dr Komoti, pointing to the north. 'You can look at the garden as much as you like.'

'You are very kind,' said Mma Ramotswe. 'Thank you.'

Mma Ramotswe spent a few minutes in the garden, then walked away. So there were two Dr Komotis. Twin brothers. But it was not unusual for two brothers to study medicine.

She drove to the railway station and stopped the van outside. She saw a woman selling food and sweet drinks.

'I am looking for a doctor called Dr Komoti,' she said. 'Do you know where his place is?'

The woman pointed to a building across a dusty square. 'Over there,' she said. 'Many people go to that doctor.'

Mma Ramotswe thanked the woman and walked across the square. The door of the building was not locked. She pushed it open and found a woman inside.

'I am sorry but the doctor isn't here, Mma,' said the woman. 'I am the nurse. You can see the doctor on Monday afternoon.'

'I just wanted to say hello to Dr Komoti,' said Mma Ramotswe. 'I worked for him when he was in Nairobi. I was a nurse in the hospital there. Do you know the other Dr Komoti? The brother?'

'Oh, yes,' said the nurse. She was more friendly now. 'He often comes in here to help. Two or three times a week.'

Mma Ramotswe put down her cup, very slowly.

'Oh, they did that up in Nairobi too,' she said carelessly. 'One doctor helped the other. And usually the patients didn't know that they were seeing a different doctor.'

The nurse laughed. 'They do it here too,' she said. 'Nobody has realised that there are two doctors. Everyone seems happy. But only one of them is a good doctor. I am surprised that the other one passed his examinations.'

Mma Ramotswe thought, but did not say, 'He didn't.'

She went back to Gaborone the next day and telephoned Dr Maketsi. He came to her office immediately.

'Dr Komoti is not taking drugs,' she said. 'But he has a twin brother. One of the brothers passed his examinations and became a doctor. The other didn't. The doctor took two jobs, here and in South Africa. When he wasn't working in the hospital, the other man, his brother, did his work for him.'

Dr Maketsi sat silent with his head in his hands.

'So we've had both doctors in our hospital,' he said. 'Only one is a real doctor, but he gets paid for two jobs. I'll have to go to the police, but this will be very bad for our hospital. People will be afraid to go there now.'

'I agree with you,' said Mma Ramotswe. 'We must protect people. Why don't we tell the police in South Africa, not the police in Gaborone. I shall telephone my friend, Billy Pilani. He is a police chief down there. It will be in the newspapers in South Africa. But people in Gaborone won't find out about it.'

'That's a very good idea,' said Dr Maketsi, smiling warmly at his old friend.

Chapter 10   The Witchdoctor's Wife

Mma Ramotswe had to find out about the schoolteacher's missing son, so she drove out to the witchdoctor's place in her tiny white van. It was in a very empty part of the country with no animals and only a few small trees.

Suddenly she saw the house by the side of a hill. She parked the van and got out. She felt afraid. She knew many different kinds of people, but this man was a murderer.

The sun was high in the sky as she walked towards the house. She felt that someone was watching her. There was a low wall around the house. At the wall, she stopped and called out.

'I am very hot,' she said loudly. 'I need water.'

There was no reply from inside the house. Mma Ramotswe heard a noise behind her, and turned round.

'Mma?'

She turned round again quickly. A woman was standing in the doorway.

A woman was standing in the doorway.

'I am Mma Ramotswe,' she said. 'I have come to see your husband. I want to ask him for something. I have heard he is a very good doctor. I have trouble with another woman. She is taking my husband from me and I want something to stop her.'

The woman smiled. 'He can help you. But he is away. He is in Lobatse until Saturday. You will have to come back.'

'This has been a long trip,' said Mma Ramotswe. 'I am thirsty. Do you have water, sister?'

'Yes, I have water. You can sit in the house while you drink it.'

Mma Ramotswe went into the house. The room inside was small, with a table and two chairs. She sat on a chair and drank the water gratefully. Then she put down the cup and looked at the woman.

'I am here because you are in danger,' she said. 'I am a typist. I work for the police. And I have typed out something about your husband. He killed that boy, the one from Katsana. He used the boy for *muti*. The police know this. They are going to catch your husband and then they will kill him. They are going to kill you too. But I don't think they should kill women. Come to the police with me now. Tell them what happened. Or you will die very soon. Next month, I think. Do you understand?' She stopped.

The woman looked at her with eyes wide with fear. 'I did not kill that boy,' she said.

'I know,' said Mma Ramotswe. 'But that doesn't make any difference to the police. The Government wants to kill you too. Your husband first, you later. They do not like witchdoctors.'

'But the boy is not dead,' said the woman quickly. 'My husband took him to the cattle farm. He is working there. He is still alive.'

Mma Ramotswe opened the door of the tiny white van and told the woman to get inside. It was one o'clock and the seats inside the van were very hot. Then they drove to the cattle farm. It was a difficult journey of about four hours across empty country. At last they saw some trees around two small buildings.

'That is the cattle farm,' said the woman. 'There are two Basarwa★ there — a man and a woman. The boy works for them.'

'How do you stop him running away?'

'Look around you,' said the woman. 'You can see how lonely this place is. If he runs away, the Basarwa will catch him easily.'

'There is a man in Gaborone who bought a bone from your husband,' said Mma Ramotswe. 'Where did you get that?'

'You can buy bones in Johannesburg,' said the woman. 'Did you not know that? They are not expensive.'

The Basarwa were eating a meal. They were tiny people with skin dry from the sun and wide eyes. They looked at the visitors in surprise. Then the man stood up.

'Are the cattle all right?' asked the witchdoctor's wife.

'All right,' said the man. 'They are not dead.'

'Where is the boy?'

'Over there,' replied the man. 'Look.'

They saw a boy standing under a tree. He was a dusty little boy, with a stick in his hand.

'Come here,' called the witchdoctor's wife. 'Come here.'

The boy walked over to them, looking at the ground. He had a deep cut on his arm.

Mma Ramotswe put a hand on his shoulder.

'What is your name?' she asked very quietly. 'Are you the teacher's son from Katsana Village?'

The boy shook with fear, but he answered. 'I am that boy. I work here now. I have to look after the cattle.'

'Did this man hit you?' asked Mma Ramotswe quietly.

★ Basarwa: probably the first people in Botswana

'All the time,' said the boy.

'You are safe now,' said Mma Ramotswe. 'You are coming with me. Right now. Walk in front of me. I will look after you.'

The boy looked at the Basarwa and then moved towards the van.

'That's right,' said Mma Ramotswe. 'I am coming too.'

She put him in the passenger seat and closed the door. Then she got into the driver's seat and started the engine.

'Wait for me!' shouted the witchdoctor's wife, but the van drove away.

Mma Ramotswe turned towards the frightened little boy.

'I am taking you home now,' she said. 'It will be a long journey.'

At Katsana Village the next day, the schoolteacher looked out of the window of his house and saw a tiny white van. He saw a woman get out of the van and look at his door. There was a child in the van. Was the woman a parent who was bringing a child to him? He went outside.

'You are the teacher, Rra?'

'I am the teacher, Mma. Can I do anything for you?'

She turned to the van and waved to the child inside. The door opened and the boy came out. The teacher cried out and ran forward. He shouted wildly for the world to hear his happiness.

Mma Ramotswe walked back towards her van. She was crying, remembering her own dead child. There was so much suffering in Africa. Sometimes you just wanted to walk away.

'But you can't do that,' she thought. 'You just can't.'

◆

There was something wrong with the tiny white van.

'It's the dust from the journey to the cattle farm,' thought Mma Ramotswe. She telephoned Tlokweng Road Speedy Cars.

'I will come to Zebra Drive and look at the van on Saturday,' said Mr JLB Matekoni.

'It is an old van,' said Mma Ramotswe. 'I will have to sell it.'

'No,' said Mr JLB Matekoni. 'Everything can be repaired.' He suddenly felt sad. 'Even a broken heart?' he thought. 'Who can repair that?'

He arrived shortly after four o'clock on Saturday.

'I'll make you a cup of tea,' said Mma Ramotswe. 'You can drink it while you look at the van.'

From the window she watched him work. She took out two cups of tea and then a third, as it was a hot afternoon. Then she went into her kitchen and put vegetables into a pot and watered the plants. It was her favourite time of day, when the afternoon was changing into evening.

She went out to see Mr JLB Matekoni. He was standing next to the little white van.

'It will be fine now,' he said. 'The engine runs well.'

Mma Ramotswe was very pleased. She went into her kitchen and poured Mr JLB Matekoni a glass of beer. They sat outside the house together. Not far away, they could hear music from another house. The sun went down, and it was dark.

He looked at her – this woman who was everything to him.

'I am very happy that I repaired your van,' he said. 'I am very happy sitting here with you.'

She turned to him. 'What did you say?'

'I said, please marry me, Mma Ramotswe. I am just Mr JLB Matekoni, that's all, but please marry me and make me happy.'

'Of course I will,' said Mma Ramotswe.

ACTIVITIES

Chapters 1–2

Before you read

1 Mma Ramotswe is a private detective in Botswana, in Africa. What other famous stories about private detectives do you know? Which detective is your favourite? Why? Where does he or she solve crimes?

2 Read the Introduction to this book.
   a Who are Mma Makutsi and Mr JLB Matekoni?
   b How does the writer, Alexander McCall Smith, know about Botswana?

3 Look at the map opposite page 1 of this book and answer these questions.
   a What is the capital of Botswana?
   b Name a river in Botswana.
   c Which countries are north and south of Botswana?
   d Which city on the map is in Zimbabwe?

4 Look at the Word List at the back of the book. Check the meanings of new words.
   a Which are words for people?
   b Which are words for animals?

5 Complete these sentences with words from the Word List.
   a I crossed the . . . . . from South Africa to Botswana.
   b It is a dangerous job, working down in the . . . .
   c After his accident, he . . . a lot of money from his . . . company.
   d She went to a job . . . to find new work.

While you read

6 Number these in the correct order, from 1 to 8.
   a Precious Ramotswe moves to Gaborone.   . . . . .
   b She marries Note Makoti.   . . . . .
   c Her father dies.   . . . . .
   d She opens the No. 1 Ladies' Detective Agency. . . . . .
   e She does her first piece of detective work.   . . . . .
   f Her father returns from the mines.   . . . . .

50

g She solves Happy Bapetsi's problem. . . . . .

h She loses her baby. . . . . .

After you read

7 Answer these questions.

    a Who helped Precious after her mother died?

    b What was Precious's first job?

    c Why did Precious decide to marry Note?

    d Why did Precious's father die?

    e What did he leave her after he died?

    f Why does Happy Bapetsi say that she has been lucky in her life?

8 Work in pairs and have this conversation.

    Student A: You are Happy Bapetsi's 'Daddy'. You have left Happy's house. Tell your friend why you went there. Explain why you had to leave. How do you feel now?

    Student B: You are the Daddy's friend. Ask him what happened in Gaborone. Tell him how you feel about his actions.

Chapters 3–4

Before you read

9 Discuss these questions.

    a What kinds of problems does a private detective have to solve in your country?

    b Why do people sometimes prefer to go to a private detective and not the police?

    c What does a private detective's secretary do?

While you read

10 Who says these words? Who are they talking to?

    a 'A woman sees more than a man.' . . . .

    . . . .

    b 'Another woman, perhaps?' . . . .

    . . . .

    c 'Are you a policeman?' . . . .

    . . . .

d 'But I have lots to do.' ....

....

e 'We can't help that poor man.' ....

....

f 'A witchdoctor has taken him.' ....

....

After you read

11 Find the correct description of each of these people.

    a Mma Makutsi   the wife of a missing man

    b Reverend Shadreck   the owner of a car repair

       Mapeli   business

    c Mma Malatsi   the father of a missing boy

    d Mr JLB Matekoni   the head of a Christian group

    e Ernest Molai Pakotati   an excellent secretary

12 Are these sentences right or wrong? Correct the mistakes.

    a The No. 1 Ladies' Detective Agency is in Zebra Drive.

    b Mma Ramotswe receives a letter about a missing husband.

    c Peter Malatsi was eaten by a crocodile.

    d The boy is the teacher's only child.

    e Mr JLB Matekoni owns a garage in Mochudi.

    f He thinks that the boy is alive.

13 Answer these questions.

    a What did Mma Ramotswe's lawyer think of her business idea?

    b How did Mma Ramotswe find a secretary?

    c Why didn't the Reverend Mapeli go to the police?

    d How does Mma Ramotswe solve the problem of the missing man?

    e What does she find inside the crocodile that makes her sure?

    f Why are the police afraid to look for the missing boy? What does Mr JLB Matekoni think?

14 Work in pairs and have this conversation..

    Student A: You are Mma Ramotswe. Telephone the head of the Botswana Secretarial College. Explain that you are looking for a good secretary. Ask questions about the most important skills of a secretary.

Student B: You are the head of the Botswana Secretarial College. Tell Mma Ramotswe about Mma Makutsi. Say why she will be the perfect secretary.

Chapters 5–6

Before you read

15 Discuss these questions.

    a Mma Ramotswe is worried about money. How can the No. 1 Ladies' Detective Agency make more money, do you think? Is Mma Ramotswe right that an office has to have a secretary?

    b Mr JLB Matekoni is Mma Ramotswe's friend. What do they do together? What is important in a friend? What favourite activities do *you* enjoy doing with your friends?

While you read

16 Who:

    a goes to an expensive private school? ....

    b is trying to protect his daughter? ....

    c lies to Mma Ramotswe? ....

    d is introduced to Mma Ramotswe a year later? ....

    e wants to protect her husband? ....

    f is a South African policeman? ....

    g steals the stolen car from Mr Pekwane? ....

    h asks Mma Ramotswe to marry him? ....

After you read

17 Choose the correct answer.

    a Mr Patel's family is from ... .
       India   Botswana   South Africa

    b Nandira goes into the bookshop with ... .
       her friend's mother   her friend   Jack

    c She ... that Mma Ramowtswe is following her.
       knows   doesn't know   is worried

    d Mma Ramotswe reads a book about ... .
       cattle   crocodiles   snakes

e Mma Ramotswe meets Jack . . . .

in a bookshop   in the cinema   at a hotel

f Mma Pekwane . . . that her husband's car is stolen.

is happy   is sure   isn't sure

g The car was stolen in . . . .

Botswana   Zambia   South Africa

h The car is returned to . . . .

its owner   Mr Pekwane   an insurance company

18 Answer these questions.

a Why doesn't Mma Pekwane go to the police about the car?

b How does Mr JLB Matekoni help Mma Ramotswe?

c How does Billy Pilani find out that the car was stolen?

d How does Mma Ramotswe get the car keys?

e Why doesn't Mma Pekwane's husband call the police when the car is taken from his house?

19 Discuss what you know about Mr JLB Matekoni. Why do you think he wants to marry Mma Ramotswe? How does Mma Ramotswe feel about him? Why?

Chapters 7–8

Before you read

20 The first story in these chapters is about an insurance claim for a missing finger. Discuss these questions.

a When do people make insurance claims? Give three examples. Have you or people in your family ever made a claim? What happened?

b How can someone lose a finger? List three ways.

21 In Chapter 8, we learn about a witchdoctor. What do you know about witchdoctors? Would you like to meet one? Why (not)?

While you read

22 Are these sentences right (✔) or wrong (✗)?

a Solomon Moretsi had an accident in Hector Lepodise's factory.   . . . . .

b Mr Moretsi has never made a claim for money before.   . . . . .

c Mma Ramotswe is bitten by a snake.   . . . . .

54

d Mr Moretsi's lawyer believed his client's story before
Mma Ramotswe's visit.   . . . . .
e Mr Moretsi has only lost one finger.   . . . . .
f Mma Ramotswe thinks that Mr Moretsi should go to
prison.   . . . . .
g A bone was found in Charlie Gotso's car.   . . . . .
h The bone is from an animal.   . . . . .
i Mr Gotso agrees that the bone is his.   . . . . .
j He tells Mma Ramotswe how she can find the
witchdoctor.   . . . . .

After you read

23 Explain what these are. Why are they important to the stories?

    a hospital reports

    b a little bag made of animal skin

24 Work in pairs. Have this conversation.

    Student A: You are Mma Ramotswe. You meet Hector Lepodise
again. Tell him what happened with Mr Moretsi.

    Student B: You are Hector Lepodise. Ask Mma Ramotswe what
happened. Tell her how you feel now. Thank her for
helping you.

25 Mr JLB Matekoni is very unhappy about telling lies. But he agrees
with Mma Ramotswe that 'murder is worse than lies.' What do you
think? Is it ever acceptable or good to tell a lie? Have you ever got
into trouble because of a lie? What happened? Discuss these
questions.

Chapters 9–10

Before you read

26 In these chapters, Mma Ramotswe solves two mysteries. Discuss
these questions.

    a In the first story, a hospital doctor sometimes does very good
work and sometimes makes terrible mistakes. What are the
possible reasons for this, do you think?

    b In Chapter 10, Mma Ramotswe visits the witchdoctor. What will
she learn? What happened to the boy? How will the story end?

While you read

27 Complete the story about Dr Komoti. Write one word in each space.

Dr Maketsi is worried that Dr Komoti takes .... Mma Ramotswe .... the doctor in her tiny white van. She can't cross the South African border the first time because she hasn't got her .... When she does visit his house in Mafikeng, she finds .... Dr Komotis. The real Dr Komoti has two jobs – one in South Africa and one in .... He is very busy, so his .... helps him with his work.

28 Who says:

   a 'I have trouble with another woman.'   ....

   b 'I did not kill that boy.'   ....

   c 'I have to look after the cattle.'   ....

   d 'You are safe now.'   ....

   e 'Everything can be repaired.'   ....

   f 'Of course I will.'   ....

After you read

29 Discuss the reasons for these actions and feelings.

   a Mma Ramotswe tells the police in South Africa, not the Botswana police, about Dr Komoti.

   b She feels happy and sad when she takes the boy back to the schoolteacher.

   c She decides to marry Mr JLB Matekoni.

30 Work in pairs. Have this conversation.

   Student A: You are Mma Ramotswe. Telephone Billy Pilani. Tell him about the two Dr Komotis. Explain why you are calling him and not the Botswana police.

   Student B: You are Billy Pilani. Ask Mma Ramotswe questions about the doctors. Tell her what you are going to do.

31 Think about the problems that Mma Ramotswe has tried to solve in this book. How successful has she been? Has she failed in any way?   .

Writing

32 Before he died, Precious Ramotswe told her Daddy about her plans for a detective agency. He died before he could answer her. Imagine the words that he wanted to say. Write the speech.

33 You are the Daddy who stayed at Happy Bapetsi's house. Write a letter to Happy. Explain why you came to her house. Tell her you are sorry.

34 Explain what happened to Mma Malatsi's husband. Write about his death.

35 Write Billy Pilani's police report about the return of the stolen car to the insurance company.

36 You are a newspaper reporter in South Africa. Write a story about the doctor with two jobs.

37 You are Mr Pakotati, the teacher in Katsana Village. Write a second letter to Mma Ramotswe. Thank her for finding your son.

38 Why does Mma Ramotswe change her mind about Mr JLB Matekoni? Is this a good ending for the book, do you think? Why (not)?

39 Write about two of these people. What are they like? Compare them.

Mma Ramotswe   Mr JLB Matekoni   Mr Patel   Charlie Gotso
Nandira Patel

40 Make a list of information that you have learnt about Botswana and the way of life there from this book.

41 What have you enjoyed most about this book? Which story did you find most interesting? Would you like to read another book about the No. 1 Ladies' Detective Agency? Why (not)?

WORD LIST

agency (n) a special kind of business

baptise (v) to accept someone into the Christian Church by a religious act. This act is called **baptism**.

bone (n) one of the hard white parts inside your body

border (n) the line between two countries

cattle (n) animals kept on a farm for their meat and milk

claim (n/v) a request for money – after an accident, for example

client (n) someone who pays for your help

crocodile (n) a large animal with a long body and a long mouth with sharp teeth that lives in rivers and lakes

drug (n) something that people take to feel happy or excited

dust (n) very small pieces of earth or sand that you can see in the air or on dry ground

engine (n) the part of a car, usually at the front, that makes the car move

insure (v) to pay money to an insurance company every year. If something bad happens to you, the company will pay the costs.

lawyer (n) someone who knows about the law. People visit him or her when they have a problem

mine (n) a deep hole under the ground where men work. They look for gold, for example

Reverend (n) the title of a person who works for the Christian Church

snake (n) an animal with a long thin body and no legs

tiny (adj) very small

twin (n/adj) one of two children born at the same time to the same mother

van (n) a small vehicle with space in the back for carrying things

witchdoctor (n) a person who makes people better with special medicine